Pick a Po

MOJO JOJO'S SECRET PAPER

by Jo Duffy

Scholastic Inc.
New York • Toronto • London • Auckland • Sydney
Mexico City • New Delhi • Hong Kong • Buenos Aires

ISBN 0-439-33265-6

Cover and interior illustrations by Christopher Cook

Inked by Michele Parrish McKnight

Designed by Mark Neston

12 11 10 9 8 7 6 5 4 3 2 1 2 3 4 5 6 7/0

Printed in the U. S. A.

First Scholastic printing, October 2002

Read This First!

Sugar...Spice...and Everything Nice...

These were the ingredients chosen to create the perfect little girl. But Professor Utonium accidentally added an extra ingredient to the concoction—Chemical X!

And thus, The Powerpuff Girls were born! Using their ultra superpowers, Blossom, Bubbles, and Buttercup have dedicated their lives to fighting crime and the forces of evil!

But now, The Powerpuff Girls need *your* help! In every Pick a Powerpuff Path, you will take on the role of one of the characters and help save the day.

Or maybe you'll help *ruin* the day, because in this book you will be Mojo Jojo, the evil monkey supervillain. Mojo's dream is to defeat The Powerpuff Girls. If he could only get some Chemical X, he'd get his own superpowers, allowing him to confront the Girls on their own terms. Better still, if he could just get his hands on the Professor's secret formula for Chemical X, he could make all the Chemical X he wanted!

Will he succeed? That's up to you! Depending on the choices you make, Mojo's story will take a different direction. When you are through reading one story, you can start over and make new choices to read a brand-new story. Mojo Jojo's sinister plot is waiting—turn the page to get going!

The city of Townsville! Home of The Powerpuff Girls! A beautiful place, where the people are friendly, and everybody feels happy. Everyone, that is, except for that miserable, evil monkey super-genius, Mojo Jojo!

Mojo Jojo looked down on Townsville from his Volcano Top Observatory as he plotted and schemed.

"Look at them, those citizens of Townsville," Mojo said, scowling into his telescope. "They ignore me, Mojo Jojo, for they are way too busy feeling happy, and thinking about how much they love their precious Powerpuff Girls to ever think of me...except when I am committing crimes.

"It is not fair," Mojo added. "The Powerpuff Girls live together in a beautiful house with their precious Professor, who also created me, but who does not give *me* a beautiful place to live. I had to design and build my own secret lair. The Girls are famous for just being themselves. I am famous only when I am brilliantly evil. Devising schemes and designing mighty weapons is hard work, even when you are brilliant and evil like me, Mojo Jojo! It isn't fair at all!"

Suddenly, Mojo had an idea. As he often did when he had an idea, he spoke it aloud, even though there was no one to hear him. "If I had my own supply of Chemical X, I would have super-powers, which would make all of my evil plotting and scheming so much easier. I think Professor Utonium owes me the formula to Chemical X. It would make up for all the times his Powerpuff Girls have embarrassed me and defeated me and thrown me in jail." Mojo was conveniently forgetting that the Girls only fought him or arrested him when he committed crimes!

Since Professor Utonium was unlikely to give the formula to Mojo Jojo, Mojo decided to go to the home of The Powerpuff Girls and steal it from the Professor's laboratory. Then, he, Mojo, could make all of the Chemical X he wanted. Mojo grabbed a few devices he thought would be useful for his theft, got into his flying car, and flew to the home of The Powerpuff Girls.

Mojo landed in the bushes and snooped around outside the Professor's lab. He waited by the window to see if it was safe to break in. Then he heard the voices of the Professor, Blossom, Buttercup, and Bubbles.

"Curses," Mojo muttered. "All of them are home. I must learn more and find out when the coast will be clear. And then I, Mojo Jojo, will steal the formula for Chemical X."

"Yes, Girls," the Professor was saying as Mojo listened. "This paper contains something very precious and important." Mojo peered inside the window and saw The Powerpuff Girls crowded around the Professor, who was indeed holding a piece of paper.

"It's kind of like a secret, isn't it, Professor?" asked Bubbles.

"Let's just say I think it needs to stay in the right hands," replied the Professor.

"Don't worry," said Blossom. "You can count on us to protect the paper."

"Yeah," Buttercup grinned. "And if any bad guys try to take it, you can count on us to stop them!"

"That's it!" said Mojo Jojo to himself. "If that paper means so much to Professor Utonium and The Powerpuff Girls, then I must steal it! In fact, I bet it contains the formula for Chemical X! Should I act now, and grab the paper before it is too late? Or is it too risky to go after the paper while the Professor and all three Powerpuff Girls are in the house?"

If Mojo decides to try to steal the paper right away, turn to page 11.

If Mojo decides to wait for a while to see if the Professor and the Girls leave the house, turn to page 8.

Mojo Jojo decided to wait. Even one Powerpuff Girl was usually strong enough to defeat him. *But once they leave,* he thought, *I will steal the formula for Chemical X, and then I will make Chemical X, and then I will have superpowers. Never again will I be defeated by little Girls who are full of the power of Chemical X, for I, too, will have the power of Chemical X! I will challenge, and then I will defeat, The Powerpuff Girls!*

Mojo settled down in the flower bed beneath the window to wait for the Girls and the Professor to leave the house, lost in a beautiful daydream of someday defeating The Powerpuff Girls.

But Mojo got a little more lost in his daydream than he intended to. Before he even realized that he had fallen asleep, Mojo was awakened by a familiar sound—that of three little Girls taking off at super-speed. He looked up in time to see Buttercup, Bubbles, and Blossom flying off in three different directions. Each of the Girls was holding a piece of paper.

Which paper contained the formula for Chemical X? Which Girl should Mojo follow?

If Mojo decides to follow Blossom, turn to page 25.

If Mojo decides to follow Buttercup, turn to page 27.

If Mojo decides to follow Bubbles, turn to page 56.

Mojo Jojo aimed his pocket laser and shattered the beaker of bright blue goo.

"Now you've done it, Mojo!" yelled the Professor, as goo and broken glass spilled onto the laboratory floor.

Something was moving on the floor! A little tadpole, flipping about in the wreckage, began to grow—bigger and bigger and bigger, until it almost filled the entire lab.

"What's that?" asked Mojo.

Professor Utonium answered, "It's a baby monster I was storing in that beaker for safety. The blue goo can keep monsters at tadpole size...until someone lets them out."

Mojo decided it was a good time to leave. The monster noticed him moving. It seemed to be delighted at the sight of him. "Play!" said the monster. "Toy! Play! Want to play now!!" It lunged forward, blocking Mojo's escape. The evil monkey supervillain was trapped!

If Mojo decides to try to chase the baby monster away, turn to page 46.

If Mojo decides to make friends with the baby monster, turn to page 52.

Mojo Jojo decided he had better take action and steal the secret paper—which he was sure contained the formula for Chemical X—right away. After all, he knew where it was now—in the Professor's laboratory. If Mojo waited, there was no telling where the Professor would hide it next. Mojo might never get this chance again.

But there were four do-gooders in the lab, and only one monkey supervillain, and three of those do-gooders were very strong and would be very angry if Mojo tried to rob them.

Would a sneaky plot—some kind of distraction, for example—or a direct challenge be the best way to steal the formula?

If Mojo decides to create a distraction, turn to page 26.

If Mojo decides to boldly challenge The Powerpuff Girls, turn to page 35.

The paper tucked into the Talking Dog's collar must be the one that Bubbles had, thought Mojo. *He is obviously hiding some valuable secret—perhaps even the formula I am after! Fortunately, this dog will be easy to defeat. He is no match for me, Mojo Jojo!*

Mojo used his flying car to hover above the Talking Dog as the little white pooch trotted to a secluded part of Townsville Park, underneath some shady trees. "Now is the time for me to strike!" Mojo said to himself. "Dogs are used to listening to commands, and surely the Talking Dog will obey any commands given by me, Mojo Jojo, monkey super-genius! Or perhaps I should just use my superior monkey brain to outwit his poor, inferior doggy mind, and trick him into giving me the secret paper!"

If Mojo decides to command the Talking Dog to give him the paper, turn to page 61.

If Mojo decides to trick the Talking Dog into giving him the paper, turn to page 54.

"A mere Talking Dog is not worth my time," Mojo Jojo said to himself. "I will follow Bubbles, for surely she still has the important secret paper. She must have given something else to that foolish canine." Mojo let Bubbles get a little bit ahead of him so that he could continue to follow her unobserved.

By the time Mojo caught up to her, Bubbles was standing on the doorstep of a building with a sign on the wall that read TOP SECRET PRIVATE CLUB. A man just inside the doorway was holding a piece of paper.

"Thank you for bringing this, Bubbles," the man said.

Mojo was confused. How many pieces of paper was Bubbles carrying with her, anyway? Was the paper the man was holding the secret paper that the Professor had spoken about, or did Bubbles still have it? What was the man thanking Bubbles for?

The evil monkey couldn't tell who had the paper he wanted. And he still didn't know what the paper he wanted said!

While Mojo was trying to make up his mind, the man went back inside the secret club and closed the door, and Bubbles flew away.

If Mojo decides to continue to follow Bubbles, turn to page 62.

If Mojo decides to enter the club, turn to page 42.

Mojo Jojo pulled out the control box for his latest model of a giant robot, which he kept stored at his Observatory when it wasn't turned on. This giant robot would obey every command that Mojo sent it through the control box, so he pressed the button that would activate and summon the robot.

"Powerpuff Girls, prepare to be defeated!" Mojo gloated, laughing and hooting like the evil monkey he was. "This is the day you will not be victorious, for I, Mojo Jojo, have summoned my new giant robot. When it arrives, it will defeat you. To save yourselves, you must give me the precious secret paper I heard you talking about!"

"No way, Mojo!" Blossom replied, zipping forward at super-speed. She grabbed the control box out of Mojo's hands and tossed it to Buttercup, who crushed it into scrap metal.

"Sorry, Mojo!" Buttercup mocked him. "I hope that wasn't anything important."

Mojo knew that destroying the control box had cut off the signal to his robot—now the robot could never find him.

"Ummm...of course not," the supervillain answered, trying to sound friendly. "Think nothing of it."

"Why did you want my precious paper?" asked Bubbles. "It was wonderful of the Professor to surprise me with an autographed picture of my favorite TV stars, the *TV Puppet Pals*! He and the Girls have been keeping the secret for weeks!"

Mojo was extremely embarrassed. He'd been plotting and scheming to get his hands on a picture of *puppets*? If any other villains ever heard about this, they would make fun of him for the rest of his life! But now, he had to find some way to get out of the Girls' house—fast!

"I, uh..." Mojo thought furiously. "I heard that sometimes the Puppet Pals accidentally misspell their own names when they autograph pictures," he stammered. "I just wanted to see if your picture is correct, because I would not want you to have an incorrectly signed picture."

Bubbles gasped. "Professor, is the picture okay?"

"It's perfect, Bubbles," the Professor reassured her. "The autographs are perfectly spelled, and the penmanship is excellent."

"Hey," said Buttercup when they were finished admiring Bubbles's treasure, "where's Mojo?"

"He jumped out the window," answered Blossom. "I think he's going home. Can't you hear the sound of his flying car?"

With their super-hearing, the Girls could hear the monkey supervillain say, "I am ashamed. I am humiliated. I can never show my face in this town again."

"What do you think *that* was all about?" wondered Buttercup aloud.

Continue on page 64.

Mojo Jojo loved listening to classical music, but performing a musical number was out of the question. He couldn't play an instrument, and he couldn't carry a tune. He decided to keep trying to bluff his way into the club, however.

"What kind of club is this?" Mojo asked.

"It's a blues club," the manager replied.

"Then I cannot, in good conscience, perform," Mojo told him, with a great show of regret. "I am an operatic star, and my brilliant singing would be out of place in a humble house of blues. I have no desire to shame my fellow performers by flaunting a talent so vastly superior to any they possess. But in gratitude for how considerately I have shielded the tender feelings of those of lesser talent than myself, perhaps you would still let me come in...."

"No!" said the bouncer and the manager at the same time.

"Not even for a minute?" asked Mojo.

"No!" the bouncer and the manager both said again.

"Not even if I beg you?" begged Mojo.

"No!" they said.

"Not even if I whine?" whined Mojo.

"You are really beginning to irritate me," said the manager.

"Then give me the paper little Bubbles brought you," Mojo pleaded, "and I'll go away. Pleeeeeeeeeease?"

"Fine!" said the manager irritably. "If it will make you go away." The manager handed Mojo a piece of paper.

"At last!" Mojo gloated, unfolding it. "At last I have the secret formula for...Super-messy Guacamole Surprise?! What the heck is *this*?"

"The Powerpuff Girls' favorite snack food," the manager answered. "The Girls perform here all the time. I promised to serve the guacamole the next time they play."

"Blues music and guacamole? I *hate* guacamole! If I wanted to steal a recipe, it would be for something good, like yummy cake with lots of icing." Mojo was outraged and frustrated. He had made himself hungry for cake, and he wanted to listen to a good, long opera far away from those guacamole-loving blues musicians.

Mojo handed the manager back his disgusting recipe, stomped off to his flying car, and headed for home.

Continue on page 64.

A few minutes later, Blossom left. "When everyone who works here goes home for the night, I will break into the Mayor's office and steal the secret paper," Mojo chuckled to himself, settling down to wait.

Finally, Mojo saw the Mayor and Ms. Bellum putting on their coats to go home.

"Good night, Mayor," Ms. Bellum said. "Do you have the paper from Professor Utonium? Remember his instructions!"

"It's right here," replied the Mayor, showing her the paper and then putting it back in his pocket.

Curses! Now I will have to follow the Mayor to get the paper! thought Mojo. *Fortunately, this foolish Mayor is no match for me, Mojo Jojo!*

"Good night, Ms. Bellum," said the Mayor, and then he sneezed.

"*Gesundheit*, Mayor," said Ms. Bellum. Then they went their separate ways. Mojo used his flying car to follow the Mayor's limousine home.

Mojo watched the Mayor greet his wife,

Mrs. Mayor. He waited while the Mayor and Mrs. Mayor cooked and ate some kind of homemade soup for dinner.

Finally, the Mayor and his wife went to bed. "Good night, dear," said Mrs. Mayor. "I hope you get a good night's sleep."

"I expect I will," said the Mayor, with a little sniff.

As soon as they were asleep, Mojo broke into the Mayor's house. He found the paper he was after in the kitchen, where the Mayor had left it. Eagerly, Mojo looked to see what it said.

"PROFESSOR UTONIUM'S TOP SECRET COLD REMEDY?!" said Mojo in disbelief.

Blossom's piece of paper didn't contain the formula for Chemical X after all! The soup the Mayor and his wife had been cooking and eating was actually a homemade chicken soup remedy, which was good for curing colds. Now the couple were upstairs getting a good night's sleep, while a tired, angry villain stood alone in their kitchen feeling like a fool!

Furiously, Mojo Jojo threw the paper down, then flew home in his car. He sneezed twice before he even got to bed. By the next morning, Mojo didn't have the formula for Chemical X or the Professor's cold remedy—he'd left that behind in the Mayor's kitchen. What he *did* have was the Mayor's cold!

Continue on page 64.

Mojo Jojo knew that Buttercup trusted Ms. Keane more than anyone else in Townsville—except for the Professor, of course. Therefore, it made sense that Buttercup would trust Ms. Keane with the secret paper. So Mojo let Buttercup fly away without following her, and considered how he would get the secret paper from Ms. Keane. Mojo wondered if he should try to trick Ms. Keane out of the paper, or simply burst in and grab what he wanted. He was, after all, so magnificent and scary, mere children (at least, ones who didn't have superpowers) would never dare stand up to him. And Ms. Keane certainly couldn't stop him.

If Mojo decides to trick Ms. Keane out of the paper, turn to page 44.

If Mojo decides to simply grab the paper, turn to page 21.

Mojo decided he would simply grab the paper. He landed his flying car and burst into the kindergarten. The children sat and stared at him.

"Attention, all you little children," Mojo declared. "I am now your master."

That was as far as he got. Every little boy and girl in Pokey Oaks suddenly got up from their seats and ran...*toward* Mojo!

The astonished supervillain couldn't imagine why, until the children began to yell. "A monkey! A pet monkey! You heard what he said. From now on, Mojo's our very own *mascot*!" They began to argue over who would play with Mojo first.

Mojo headed for the door...but before he could get away, a couple of the faster kids grabbed him, and the villain was overwhelmed.

"Unhand me," Mojo yelled as the children climbed all over him, pinning him to the ground. "I said master, not mascot! Do you not know who I—*aah!* Help!"

Ms. Keane paid no attention to Mojo's shouts. She had her back turned to the class, because she was busy pinning onto the bulletin board the pretty drawing Buttercup had just delivered. The drawing had been colored by all three Powerpuff Girls, to surprise their teacher for her birthday.

With no one to rescue Pokey Oaks' reluctant new mascot from his playmates, Mojo couldn't escape from the classroom until naptime!

Continue on page 64.

Mojo Jojo aimed his pocket laser at the beaker of red goo. The beaker burst on the lab floor, and a cloud of gas billowed up. Mojo began to laugh. "Look at how funny that is," he chuckled. "All red and sparkly, which is very funny, when it is sparkly and red." Some of the gas cloud got sucked up Mojo's nose, and he laughed even harder.

The Powerpuff Girls and the Professor were laughing, too.

"You see what I have done to your experiment?" Mojo hooted. "I am sure you are sorry now that I have broken your experiment, so you should not be happy."

The Professor and the Girls laughed even harder. "It's my latest invention, a gel that turns into a cloud of laughing gas when air touches it," said

the Professor. "Its formula is on that paper you were after. The joke is on you, Mojo!"

"So it is," the evil monkey mastermind agreed. "A hilarious joke at which I will chuckle and guffaw whenever I am reminded of it...like right now. Good-bye, Professor. Good-bye, Girls! *Hoo-hoo! Hee-hee!*"

Mojo Jojo walked past the three giggling Powerpuff Girls. He got into his flying car and headed for home. When he was almost there, the joke didn't seem so funny anymore. Then he realized what had happened. "I was tricked into laughing when I inhaled the Professor's gas cloud! I was defeated through scientific deception! Curses!"

Continue on page 64.

Mojo Jojo decided that the safest thing to do at this point was to get away. Once he was safe in his lair, he could come up with some scheme to steal the secret paper. So he waited until the bouncer was busy explaining what was going on to the club manager. While the bouncer was distracted, the monkey mastermind managed to yank his cape free, run to his flying car, and zoom away.

Mojo was so conceited that soon he had convinced himself that successfully running away from a bunch of angry clubgoers was a glorious victory, and proof of the brilliance of his giant monkey brain. Mojo ignored the fact that he still hadn't figured out how he would get the secret paper. "Well done," he congratulated himself.

Then The Powerpuff Girls flew up and grabbed him.

"Curse you, Powerpuff Girls," Mojo growled. "How did you find me?"

"Simple," Buttercup told him. "We got an emergency call from the man who owns the club. He told us you tried to steal the party invitation that Bubbles dropped off for his little girl."

Mojo indignantly protested. "Invitation? That's not fair! I would never have tried to steal the paper if I had known it was a mere...um...I mean..."

Realizing too late that he should have kept his mouth shut, Mojo sighed as he was carried off to jail by the Girls.

Continue on page 64.

Blossom is the leader of The Powerpuff Girls, thought Mojo. *Surely she is the one the Professor would trust with his secret paper. I will follow her.*

Mojo zoomed after Blossom in his flying car. He stayed a little way behind her so that she wouldn't spot him.

Blossom flew to City Hall. Mojo sneaked up to the window in his car and peered into the Mayor's office. He watched Blossom give a piece of paper to the Mayor, who put the paper on his desk.

"There you are, Mayor," Blossom said. "The Professor wanted me to warn you to be very careful with these instructions. They are very important."

Why would the Professor give the Mayor the formula for Chemical X? wondered Mojo. *Well, even if that paper is not the formula I am after, it is clearly worth stealing! But how should I do it?*

If Mojo decides to steal the paper after everyone has left the Mayor's office, turn to page 18.

If Mojo decides to boldly demand that they give him the paper, turn to page 28.

If Mojo decides to kidnap the Mayor so that Mojo can trade the Mayor for the paper, turn to page 50.

Mojo Jojo decided that creating a distraction would be the best—and safest—way to steal the formula. He sorted through the gadgets he had brought with him. "Hmmm," he said to himself as he considered what to do. "A dog whistle so secret even dogs can't hear it? No. An evil joy buzzer that spreads misery to all who touch it? No. A miniature smoke machine that creates a cover of thick, dark smoke wherever it is aimed... Hmmm. Do I have my smoke-penetrating super-goggles? Yes! The smoke machine it is."

Chuckling at his own cleverness, the villainous monkey put on his goggles and aimed the smoke machine at the open lab window. As the smoke began to spread, Mojo climbed boldly inside.

"Girls, what's going on?" asked the Professor.

"I don't know, Professor," answered Bubbles. "I can't see!"

"We can take care of that," said Blossom. "Quick, Girls. Use your super-breath."

Immediately, Blossom, Buttercup, and Bubbles began to blow, sending all of the smoke back out the window. As the smoke cleared, Mojo Jojo stood revealed in front of The Powerpuff Girls and the Professor.

"It's Mojo!" yelled Buttercup. "I should have known! Let's get him!"

Mojo was caught in the act. What could he do next?

If Mojo decides to confront The Powerpuff Girls, turn to page 14.

If Mojo decides to try to talk the Girls out of getting him, turn to page 36.

"Buttercup is the toughest Powerpuff Girl," Mojo said. "Surely she is the one the Professor would trust to protect his important secrets."

Mojo Jojo tailed Buttercup through Townsville in his flying car. He saw her fly in the window of Pokey Oaks Kindergarten, where The Powerpuff Girls went to school. Mojo landed next to the window of the school and looked inside.

He saw Buttercup giving a piece of paper to her teacher, Ms. Keane.

"Thank you for taking the trouble to bring this to me," said Ms. Keane.

"You're welcome, Ms. Keane," Buttercup replied. "I'm sorry my sisters and I can't be in school today. I have to go now and save the day."

"I understand, Buttercup," said Ms. Keane. "Some emergencies call for a superhero...or three. Be careful, and I'll see you tomorrow. Good-bye."

Now that Buttercup had handed the secret paper to Ms. Keane, it was time for Mojo to strike and take the paper for himself. But was the paper Buttercup had given Ms. Keane really the secret paper the Professor had been talking about? Perhaps Buttercup had spotted him, and had given Ms. Keane a different piece of paper in order to throw him off the trail.

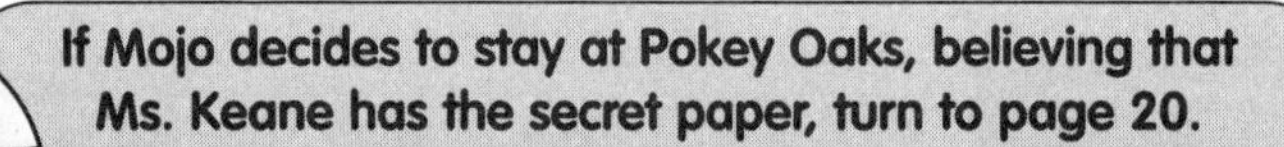

If Mojo decides to stay at Pokey Oaks, believing that Ms. Keane has the secret paper, turn to page 20.

If Mojo decides to keep following Buttercup, believing that she still has the secret paper, turn to page 38.

Mojo Jojo decided that a bold approach was best. He tethered his flying car to the window ledge and leaped through the window right into the Mayor's office.

"Oh, no!" yelled the Mayor. "It's Mojo Jojo! Help me!"

"Oh, brother," grumbled Blossom, rolling her eyes.

"Yes, be afraid, Mayor!" Mojo laughed evilly. "Give me the secret paper that Blossom gave you or you will learn how powerful and evil I truly am!"

"Let's go, Mayor," Ms. Bellum urged, grabbing the Mayor by his arm and hurrying him toward the door. "Blossom can handle Mojo more easily if she doesn't have to worry about our safety!"

"Right you are, Ms. Bellum. Thanks!" Blossom called, as the door closed behind her two friends. Then Blossom turned back to face Mojo, who had been caught by surprise when the people he wanted to scare had run away.

"Now the only one here who has anything to be afraid of is *you*, Mojo," Blossom added sternly.

Mojo could still see the secret paper on the Mayor's desk, but Blossom was blocking his way to it. How was Mojo going to get the paper now?

If Mojo decides to challenge Blossom, turn to page 34.

If Mojo decides to try to outsmart Blossom, turn to page 29.

Mojo decided he was smart enough to trick one little Girl. He said, "I cannot leave yet. Not without the secret paper I am looking for."

"What secret paper?" asked Blossom, who wasn't fooled a bit.

"A letter from my dear old granny," Mojo told her. "She told me she sent one, but even though I have waited for many days, it has not yet come. Because her letters are always personal and private, they are always labeled SECRET on the outside. I am afraid the letter has been delivered to the wrong address. So I have been asking all of my dear friends, like the Mayor, to see if they got my personal, private, secret letter by mistake."

Blossom laughed at this obvious fib. "I don't think you'll find your letter here, Mojo," she said. "The only piece of paper in here that's labeled secret is the Professor's super-secret sugar cookie recipe. I brought it here because the Professor promised to lend it to the Mayor and Ms. Bellum."

A cookie recipe? *That* was the paper he had been trying to track down and steal? Disgusted, Mojo left the Mayor's office and headed for home.

Blossom didn't bother to follow Mojo, since he hadn't actually committed any crimes. Instead, she went to tell the Mayor and Ms. Bellum that they could return to City Hall.

Continue on page 64.

Mojo Jojo decided he had better send the Talking Dog away and dig up the treasure himself. He didn't want anybody nearby to share—or steal—the loot when he finally got his paws on the treasure, especially if that treasure turned out to be Chemical X! If Chemical X could turn an ordinary little monkey into a brilliant supervillain, and create three pint-size superheroes, there was no telling how powerful it might make a dog who could already talk.

"Oh, dear!" said Mojo, acting very sympathetic. "I think I hear the dogcatcher coming right now!"

The Talking Dog looked extremely worried.

"Maybe he doesn't know you are here," Mojo suggested encouragingly.

The Talking Dog looked more cheerful.

Mojo added, "If he can't find you, then he can't take you to the pound! Run and hide, and do not talk to anyone for the rest of the day. If anyone asks, I will say I never saw you!"

The Talking Dog was completely fooled. He nodded at Mojo, looking very grateful, and then he trotted quietly away.

Mojo dug in the indicated spot, deeper and deeper and deeper...until he came upon the Talking Dog's treasure: a filthy bone covered in dog slobber! The secret paper was a map the Professor had made to help the Talking Dog stop losing his favorite bone!

Mojo was very embarrassed. He had worked and schemed and plotted, all for nothing. Even worse,

he was afraid someone might see and laugh at him. To be on the safe side, he buried the Talking Dog's treasure right where he had found it and wearily headed for home. Somehow, someone had made a fool of him again, and Mojo suspected that that someone had been himself!

Continue on page 64.

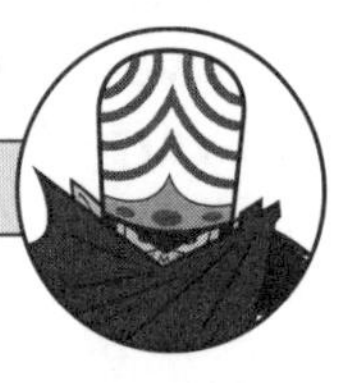

Mojo Jojo wasn't much of a musician, but he was sure that there was nothing he couldn't do—including performing a musical number. "What kind of music would you like to hear?" he asked.

"The blues," the club manager replied. "It is the best way for a man—or a monkey, or a cute little Powerpuff Girl—to express the innermost depths of sorrow. Bubbles was here before, and she brought me sheet music to a blues song she wrote. She and the Talking Dog are going to perform it tomorrow."

Mojo was very interested in what the manager had said. It sounded like the blues was his kind of music! The fact that Mojo had spent an entire frustrating day chasing the wrong piece of paper made him feel even more ready to sing the blues.

"Deep inner sorrow," Mojo said, "is something a supervillain understands very well. Lead me to the stage."

When Mojo got up onstage, he stood in front of the microphone and sang a brand-new song. He called it the "I am an Evil Genius Supervillain, Yet I Keep Getting Defeated by Sassy-Mouthed Little Girls" blues.

The audience loved it. They cheered for Mojo, demanding encore after encore. Mojo was the hit of the night.

Afterward, Mojo stayed to listen to the other musicians sing and to accept their admiring compliments and sympathy over what a hard life he'd had.

In fact, Mojo had such a wonderful time that he forgot all about his plan to steal the formula for Chemical X.

Continue on page 64.

Mojo Jojo decided to challenge Blossom. He still had a few sneaky tricks up his sleeve. He started to pull out a device from his cape.

But before he could even aim it, Blossom said, "Oh no you don't!" and froze Mojo Jojo with a blast of her ice breath.

The monkey super-genius glared at her, but he was too cold to move.

"These little confrontations of ours are getting old, Mojo," said Blossom. "The Powerpuff Girls never lose—why do you even bother? I won't put you in jail this time, but you're going home!" And Blossom picked up the ice-encrusted supervillain, flew him back to his Volcano Top lair, and left him, frozen solid, in the middle of his living room.

"The one thing I don't get," Blossom said to Mojo as she was turning to leave, "is why you were so determined to steal the Professor's designs for a new lighting system for City Hall."

Continue on page 64.

Mojo Jojo decided it was better to boldly challenge the Girls. "I am so magnificent and evil," he told himself, "and Professor Utonium and The Powerpuff Girls will be so shocked to see me in their very home that they will give me what I want just so I will leave them in peace."

Mojo leaped through the window, but before he could even complete one good burst of menacing laughter, the Professor interrupted him.

"Mojo Jojo! The worst assistant I ever had. I thought I threw you out for good! What are you *doing* in my lab?"

Mojo was offended by the interruption and by what the Professor had said about him. "Never mind," Mojo muttered. "Give me the secret paper I heard you discussing, and I will leave."

"No way," replied Buttercup.

"You can't have it!" Bubbles gasped.

"Why do you want it, anyway?" asked Blossom.

Things weren't turning out the way Mojo had expected. How could he make the Girls give up the paper? Perhaps his newest giant robot would be capable of defeating the Girls. Or maybe he should start wrecking the Girls' beautiful home. Surely the Girls would give Mojo the paper to stop him from ruining their house.

If Mojo decides to summon his giant robot, turn to page 14.

If Mojo decides to start wrecking the Girls' house, turn to page 51.

Mojo considered trying to make a run for it, but he knew that The Powerpuff Girls could easily use their super-speed to catch him. He decided instead to try to delay their chase of him with a clever lie. Maybe he could convince them not to chase him at all!

"Why, what am I doing here?" he asked, trying to sound innocent. "I was in my observatory, minding my own business, when someone turned on a smoke machine, and everything became very dark. I could not see a thing, so I went looking for the light switch, but I went too far, and wound up here, which is not my home. Thank you for blowing the smoke away, Girls," he added, moving closer to the window with every word. "Good-bye!"

"'Someone' turned on a smoke machine, huh, Mojo?" Buttercup scoffed.

"I think we know who that *someone* is," Blossom added. "Get him, Girls!"

Instantly, the supervillain was caught.

"What were you after this time anyway, Mojo?" Buttercup wondered.

"I told you, I did not mean to come here," Mojo protested.

"You know that we don't believe you, Mojo," said Bubbles. "Just tell us what's going on!"

Mojo sighed and replied, "I must have the secret paper I saw you all gloating over, for I am certain it is the formula for Chemical X."

"Wrong again, Mojo!" Buttercup laughed.

"It's actually an ad for a new book on good manners," Bubbles explained. "The Professor wants to give it to the Mayor so that he can learn how to be extra-polite when important visitors come to City Hall."

"You could use a lesson in manners yourself, Mojo," Buttercup added. "Don't you know it's not polite to break into other people's homes? We'd better fly you to jail...where we'll knock politely on the front door and ask the warden to *please* lock you away!"

Continue on page 64.

Mojo Jojo coasted through the playground of Pokey Oaks, and suddenly noticed that Buttercup and Bubbles were together again. The two Girls were having a whispered conversation. Mojo flew closer so he could overhear what they were saying.

One word reached him very clearly. It was his own name: Mojo Jojo. Bubbles and Buttercup were whispering things about him!

Mojo was so annoyed, he flew right up to them. "What is it that you are whispering about me? You must stop whispering things about me, you sassy little Girls," Mojo scolded. "I am your enemy. I am a super-genius! And I, Mojo Jojo, your enemy and super-genius, deserve respect! Instead of giving me the respect that I deserve, you have been leading me on a wild-goose chase all over Townsville, and now you are whispering things about me! You must tell me what you are whispering about!"

"Didn't anyone tell you?" asked Bubbles.

"Don't you know?" wondered Buttercup. "You better go home right now, Mojo."

"What is it that someone should tell me? I do not know what it is you are saying!" Mojo said, completely confused. "And why should I go home? I will go home when I understand what it is that you are saying about me, Mojo Jojo!"

"I guess we've got to show you what's going on," said Bubbles. She and Buttercup pulled the evil monkey right out of his car and flew him back to the park where his Volcano Top Observatory stood. The Professor and Blossom were waiting for them there.

"Good work, Girls," said the Professor. "You made sure that Mojo Jojo was safe."

"Safe? Why do you Girls think you were keeping me, Mojo Jojo, safe?" Mojo demanded.

Blossom answered, "We were checking to make sure that you weren't at home. The Professor read an important scientific paper earlier today which predicted that one of the most interesting, earth-shaking events in Townsville's history was about to occur. Bubbles, Buttercup, and I delivered copies of the paper to all of the most important people in town, and then we came to the park to keep everyone away from the event—it's happening right over there." And she indicated the volcano upon which Mojo's lair was located. The side of the volcano was erupting, spewing flames and dangerous lava everywhere. Mojo was aghast. He was about to lose his home!

"Too bad, Mojo," Buttercup gloated.

"It's very sad," Bubbles said sympathetically. "Now you have no home to go to."

"You know, Girls," the Professor said, "you should really take care of that volcano before it ruins the park!"

"You're right, Professor," said Blossom. "Let's go, Girls!"

Instantly, The Powerpuff Girls went into action. Blossom used her ice breath to freeze the flow of hot lava, cooling it into stone. Bubbles and Buttercup

Continue on page 40.

used chunks of stone to block up the cracks in the side of the volcano. In minutes, the eruption was over.

"Not bad, Girls," said the Professor, proudly.

"See you later, Mojo," Bubbles added. "It's time for us to go home!" And she and Blossom carried the Professor safely away.

"Nice place you have here, Mojo," Buttercup laughed. "You'll have to give us a tour sometime." Then Buttercup zoomed away, too.

And so, Mojo Jojo's observatory was saved—except that it was now covered in cooling lava!

Continue on page 64.

The Powerpuff Girls grabbed Mojo Jojo.

"Unhand me, you—you—you disrespectful children!" Mojo demanded. The Powerpuff Girls ignored Mojo's command.

"You've been very bad, Mojo!" Bubbles scolded him.

"And you know what happens when you've been very bad," Blossom added.

"Yeah," said Buttercup. "Time for you to move back to your second home—the Townsville Jail!"

The Girls flew Mojo Jojo through the air at a dizzying speed and dumped him into his usual jail cell. It looked exactly the same as he'd last seen it...a week before.

Continue on page 64.

Mojo Jojo was tired of chasing Bubbles all over Townsville. He thought he would try to find out just what was on the paper the man in the club had been holding. So Mojo got out of his car and walked up the steps to the club. He pounded on the door with all of his strength. "Open up in there! At once!" Mojo yelled, as loudly as he could.

The clubhouse door flew open with such force that Mojo stumbled backward. A man came out—a big, angry-looking man. He was the tallest person Mojo had ever seen, and he looked very strong. The man had muscles everywhere—and some of those muscles had muscles of their own!

"What do you want?" the man yelled.

Mojo was a bit scared of the angry, muscular man, but he decided that if he acted tough, he might be able to bluff his way into the club.

"I demand to come in," Mojo Jojo replied.

"Well, you can't! I'm the bouncer, and it's my job to *bounce* anyone who isn't invited to the club out of here!"

Mojo wondered what to do.

If Mojo decides to try to squeeze past the bouncer, turn to page 43.

If Mojo decides to find out how to get invited to the club, turn to page 53.

Mojo Jojo decided to try to squeeze past the bouncer. After all, a man who was so big and covered with bulky muscles probably couldn't move very quickly. Dashing forward as fast as he could, Mojo tried to slip into the club.

Instead, the bouncer yelled, "Not so fast!" and dragged Mojo back by his cape.

"Let go!" Mojo yelled. "You are tearing my lovely purple cape!"

"Your cape wouldn't tear if you'd stop trying to get loose," said the bouncer.

"You shouldn't have grabbed me," said Mojo angrily.

"You shouldn't have tried to sneak in," replied the bouncer just as angrily.

"Forget the club," said Mojo furiously. "I don't care about the club. It's a stupid club. I just want the secret paper I saw Bubbles bring someone inside the club! Give the paper to me now! I insist. And stop pulling on my cape!"

The angry, trapped villain yelled and squirmed so much that the bouncer called for help. Soon, everyone who was in the club came outside, including the club manager, who was the man Mojo had seen before with Bubbles. Mojo was completely surrounded.

If Mojo decides he'd better try to run away, turn to page 24.

If Mojo decides to keep trying to get the paper, turn to page 48.

Mojo Jojo decided to trick Ms. Keane out of the secret paper—if he just grabbed the paper, the kids in the classroom might get scared, and then they might start to cry. There was nothing Mojo hated more than the sound of crying little brats! So Mojo pulled a hypnosis ring out of his pocket and strolled right into the classroom.

"What are you doing here, Mojo Jojo?" asked Ms. Keane.

"I am here because I am...your secret admirer," Mojo replied. "And perhaps you would like to admire my ring!" He flashed his hand under the teacher's nose. Ms. Keane, who was very polite, looked at it carefully. In a moment, she was in a deep trance, and Mojo had her in his power. He ordered Ms. Keane to instruct all of her students to stay in their seats and be quiet while she spoke with her guest.

Mojo then commanded Ms. Keane to give him the paper Buttercup had brought her. Ms. Keane promised to obey at once. Mojo was very happy, until Ms. Keane handed him a notebook. It was Ms. Keane's entire class book, which contained her notes about the skills and development of every student in her kindergarten class.

Tucked into the binding was the paper Mojo had seen Buttercup give to Ms. Keane. It was Ms. Keane's quarterly report on how well Blossom, Buttercup, and Bubbles were doing. The Girls had brought it home for the Professor to sign.

"I don't understand," the indignant supervillain complained. "Why would a mere class report be a precious secret?"

"It's precious to the Professor because he is so proud of how well the Girls are doing," Ms. Keane, who was still hypnotized, told him. "And it's secret because the Girls didn't want any of their other friends to feel jealous. It was important that I get this back today, because the Professor had to miss our parent/teacher meeting to go to an important scientific conference, while the Girls had to skip school to stop the bank from being robbed again."

Mojo was angry at having wasted so much of his valuable time just so he could hear The Powerpuff Girls being praised again! He released Ms. Keane from his hypnotic trance. But before he could give her back her notebook, a group of parents entered the classroom. They were there for the parent/teacher meetings.

"Look!" someone yelled. "It's that nasty supervillain, Mojo Jojo! And he's got the teacher's notebook!"

"Maybe he's stealing it," someone else suggested.

A third parent added, "Or maybe he's going to write bad things about our children and ruin their futures!"

"Come on, let's get the notebook!" someone else yelled, and the crowd charged forward, all grabbing for it. Mojo dropped the notebook, ran to his flying car, and headed for home to hide out in safety.

Continue on page 64.

Mojo decided to try to chase the monster away. He pulled out another of his inventions that he'd hoped would be useful against the Girls—a machine that caused people to feel ticklish.

"This device works on many different frequencies," Mojo said to himself. "There must be one that will make the monster ticklish...and if the monster is distracted, it won't bother me! I will keep turning the dial until I find a frequency that works!"

As Mojo turned the dial, he felt ticklish himself for a moment. Then the Professor suddenly laughed. Then all three Girls giggled at once. Mojo adjusted the frequency until the Professor and the Girls calmed down. Then the monster began to shake and try to scratch itself.

"It works," Mojo gloated. "The monster will not bother me while it is distracted by feeling ticklish."

But things didn't go quite the way Mojo expected. He was still stuck in the same room as a ticklish monster, and that monster was rapidly becoming upset. The monster began jumping around, trying to make the sensation stop, and Mojo was nearly squashed. The villain quickly turned his tickle machine off. It didn't help. The monster was so animated, it went right on jumping even after Mojo turned off the machine.

"You know, Mojo," the Professor told him, "that paper you wanted was notes I've been studying on how to keep a monster calm. If you had asked me, I could have told you that trying to tickle it wouldn't work. But since the monster might

accidentally hurt someone now, I guess we'll have to send the poor thing home. Girls?"

In a flash, Blossom, Buttercup, and Bubbles caught the poor, excited, jumping monster and flew it back to its home on Monster Isle. On the way there, Bubbles told the monster not to worry, because she was sure that once it was safely back where it belonged, it would feel much better. Afterward, the Girls headed for home—and for Mojo Jojo!

Continue on page 41.

Mojo Jojo decided he had to have that paper, no matter what the cost, so he reached into his pocket and rummaged around until he found what he needed. He pulled a scary-looking, complicated control device from his pocket and pointed it at the club, saying that since everyone was outside by then anyway, he would destroy the building unless the manager handed over the paper and let him leave.

The club members were afraid their club would be destroyed by the fearsome-looking device. The bouncer released his hold on Mojo Jojo, and everyone backed away.

Nobody realized that the villain was bluffing. He was frightening them all with the remote control from his home entertainment system.

"You can't destroy my club," the manager yelled. "Powerpuff Girls! Help!"

"Oh, no!" Mojo groaned.

The Powerpuff Girls heard the cry for help and flew to the rescue.

They took Mojo's frightening-looking remote, and reassured everyone else that it was safe to go back inside the club.

"Cool remote, Mojo," Blossom remarked. "I wonder if it would work on *our* TV?"

"I wonder if it was a good idea to keep Mojo from destroying a karaoke club," Buttercup added.

"I'm glad he didn't destroy it, and the Professor will be, too," Bubbles said. "I love karaoke, even if you don't, Buttercup. I was here just a little while ago, with something the Professor wanted me to drop off: a playlist of his favorite songs for the club's next open-mike night."

Continue on page 41.

Mojo Jojo decided that the best way to get the paper would be to trade it for something that Blossom would find valuable, such as the Mayor. He parked the flying car on the window ledge and leaped through the window of the Mayor's office.

"Do not move!" Mojo yelled loudly. The Mayor and Ms. Bellum were so startled by Mojo's noisy and dramatic entrance that they stayed right where they were, just as Mojo had ordered.

Mojo turned to Blossom. "You should not move, either," he warned her. "For I am going to kidnap the Mayor, and you cannot stop me!"

Mojo was so busy yelling and giving orders that he overlooked one very important thing. He hadn't brought anything with him he could use to capture the Mayor or to threaten anyone in any way at all.

Blossom noticed, though, and she giggled. Acting very innocent, she replied, "Okay, Mojo, anything you say."

While Mojo wasn't looking, Blossom winked and smiled at Ms. Bellum, to make sure Ms. Bellum knew that she could handle Mojo.

"Now, I will depart," Mojo announced. "And I will be kidnapping the Mayor as of this moment, unless you give me the secret paper that Blossom brought here!"

The Mayor looked very worried. "Blossom, help! Don't let Mojo take me!" he yelped.

Continue on page 60.

Mojo Jojo hated it when anything bad happened to the Volcano Top Observatory where he made his home. The Professor and the Girls probably wouldn't want anything bad to happen to their home, either.

So Mojo pulled a pocket laser out of his cape. "Give me the secret paper at once," he demanded, "or I will ruin your home! And I don't mean by rearranging your furniture in an ugly arrangement!"

"Oh, yeah?" scoffed Buttercup. "I'll bet you're bluffing!"

"You wouldn't dare!" Blossom added.

"You wouldn't mess up our house!" Bubbles agreed.

"Oh, no?" Mojo laughed. "Time for a little demonstration, then. Where should I start?"

If Mojo decides to start by wrecking the experiments in the Professor's lab, turn to page 58.

If Mojo decides to go upstairs and start wrecking the living room furniture, turn to page 63.

It seemed as if the baby monster liked Mojo. Mojo was sure that with his genius, he could find a way to make a good friend of the baby. Then it would do whatever he wanted.

"If you want to play with me, I can teach you the rules to many wonderful games," the supervillain promised smoothly.

"Play?" asked the monster. "With me?"

"Yes," agreed Mojo. "We can play 'rob the bank' together. And 'wreck Townsville!' And especially 'help Mojo Jojo take over the world!' I can tell that a lovely, smart baby monster like yourself would enjoy my games."

"Play with baby? Love baby?" asked the monster. It was too young to understand most of Mojo's speech.

"Of course! I would love to play with baby," Mojo agreed.

"Mama," the monster said. "Love baby? Baby love mama! Pretty mama!"

Then the monster happily swept the astonished monkey up in its arms!

Mojo demanded to be put down, but the monster carried the objecting supervillain off into the night. As they headed for Monster Isle, Mojo could hear the Professor saying, "It's a shame Mojo and the monster left so soon. I think Mojo would have done a lot better if he could have read this article I just wrote—all about the care and feeding of baby monsters!"

Continue on page 64.

Clearing his throat, Mojo Jojo decided to try a new approach. "May I speak with the manager?" Mojo asked. "I wish to talk with him about an important matter."

The bouncer glared at Mojo suspiciously. Then the bouncer said, "Wait here," and went inside the club. In a few minutes, the bouncer came back outside with the manager—the man Mojo had seen holding the piece of paper and talking to Bubbles. A couple of other people had come outside as well, to see what was going on.

"You must invite me into your club, manager of the club," said Mojo. "I am Mojo Jojo, a powerful and evil villain. It is easier to bow to my will than to face my wrath."

"We don't care who you are," the manager replied. "This is a private club for musicians, and only musicians may come in."

Mojo thought this over. "In that case," he lied, "I must tell you that I am also a musician like yourselves. I wish to join your club. *Now* may I come in?"

"Any musician can join the club and come in," said the manager, "just as soon as he goes onstage and performs a musical number for us."

If Mojo decides to perform a musical number, turn to page 32.

If Mojo decides not to perform a musical number, turn to page 16.

Mojo Jojo decided it would be simpler to trick the Talking Dog out of the secret paper. After all, it was possible that the Talking Dog was a bad dog—and didn't listen to commands! Mojo realized that the first thing he would have to do is prevent the Talking Dog from calling The Powerpuff Girls for help. That meant he would have to stop the Talking Dog from talking! Mojo landed his flying car behind some bushes, got out of the car, rushed up to the Talking Dog, and said, "Has anyone warned you yet?"

"Warned me about what?" asked the Talking Dog, who was very trusting.

"The dogcatcher is after you," said Mojo. "He says that it is wrong that you have been running around loose, and he is going to put you in the pound. However, the dogcatcher is new in town, and he is not sure what you look like. All he knows is that you talk."

"That's okay," said the Talking Dog. "Now that you've warned me, all I have to do to keep him from getting me is not talk...oops. Uh-oh!"

"Exactly!" Mojo agreed. "Unless someone can convince the new dogcatcher to leave you alone, you cannot say another word! But perhaps if the dogcatcher does find you," Mojo added, "he will leave you alone if your license is in order. Let me check it for you."

Pretending to think that the mysterious paper was the Talking Dog's license, Mojo "borrowed" it and took a good look.

"Why, this isn't your license at all," said Mojo. "It looks like a map, showing the location of some precious secret. Maybe we had better make sure your secret is safe from the dogcatcher, too. You lead the way, and I'll follow!"

The poor Talking Dog was afraid to argue. He didn't want the dogcatcher to put him in the pound, so he showed Mojo where his own private treasure was buried.

Mojo Jojo was delighted. The map had a large X marked on it, showing where to dig for the treasure—perhaps that X was a clue that the treasure was a bottle of Chemical X!

If Mojo decides to dig up the treasure himself, turn to page 30.

If Mojo decides to make the Talking Dog dig up the treasure, turn to page 59.

"Bubbles is so cute and innocent," Mojo muttered to himself. "No one would ever suspect that the Professor would trust her to protect his important secret formula. Therefore, I am sure she is the Girl who has it. I will follow Bubbles."

Mojo was careful to keep his flying car far enough behind Bubbles so that she didn't realize he was following her.

Bubbles flew all over Townsville before she finally landed. Mojo saw her having a conversation with the Talking Dog. Bubbles wasn't holding the piece of paper anymore. Mojo was furious. Had she hidden it while he was trying to catch up with her? *Curses!* Mojo thought.

Mojo activated the spy sensors in his flying car so that he could see Bubbles and the Talking Dog more clearly—and eavesdrop on their conversation.

"You're welcome," Bubbles was saying to the Talking Dog. "We're happy to help you keep your secret hidden."

"A-ha," Mojo said. "No doubt she is talking about the paper! Maybe the Talking Dog is going to hide the paper right now. Or maybe the paper does not contain a formula at all. Perhaps it is a map that tells where to find the mysterious, valuable, hidden thing Bubbles is talking about."

Mojo noticed that the Talking Dog had a piece of paper tucked into his collar, but the paper was folded up. Mojo couldn't tell if it was the same paper he was after. While he was trying to decide, Bubbles took off.

"Good-bye, Bubbles. Thanks again for your help!" called the Talking Dog.

Mojo wasn't sure what to do. Had Bubbles taken the paper with her, or did the Talking Dog have it?

If Mojo decides to stay with the Talking Dog, turn to page 12.

If Mojo decides to keep following Bubbles, turn to page 13.

Mojo Jojo decided it would be more satisfying to destroy scientific experiments than the furnishings of an ordinary home. He waved his pocket laser around the laboratory and laughed. "So, Professor, are you working on some new device to help the world today? Something that would benefit people everywhere? It would be a shame if all of your work were for nothing!"

"Stop him, Girls," said the Professor. "But be careful! If you fight him, things will get broken, and my experiments are too important to destroy!"

"So give me the paper now," Mojo demanded, "and then nothing will get broken."

"No!" the Professor replied stoutly.

"Then maybe you need a demonstration," Mojo threatened. On the other side of the lab, Mojo spotted two interesting-looking beakers full of colored goo.

If Mojo decides to break the beaker of red goo, turn to page 22.

If Mojo decides to break the beaker of blue goo, turn to page 10.

Mojo Jojo looked with satisfaction at the spot where the treasure was buried. Mojo decided that he was too superior to do something as lowly as digging up the treasure himself, and besides, dogs were famous for being good diggers, just as he, Mojo Jojo, was famous for being a supervillain.

"I command you to dig up the treasure for me," Mojo ordered. The Talking Dog started to dig, and then stopped.

"What is it you are waiting for?" asked Mojo angrily. "I do not intend to wait here all day. I have told you to dig, and so you must dig!"

The Talking Dog clearly wanted to say something in response, but he was still afraid to talk. Instead, he tried sign language and charades, but he wasn't very good at doing either.

"Whatever is on your mind, just spit it out," Mojo said. "The dogcatcher is not really after you. I lied about the entire thing so that you would reveal your secret to me, Mojo Jojo, greatest of all supervillains!"

"Help!" the Talking Dog yelled right away. "Powerpuff Girls, help me! Mojo Jojo wants to steal the map Professor Utonium drew to help me find where I buried my tasty bone!"

"Curses!" Mojo whispered.

He heard the unmistakable sounds of three angry superpowered little Girls zooming his way, so he ducked and closed his eyes.

Continue on page 41.

"Blossom cannot help you, Mayor," Mojo Jojo warned. "I've got you now," he added, lunging for the Mayor. The Mayor backed away from Mojo, and Ms. Bellum suddenly began yelling.

Mojo stopped and glared at Ms. Bellum. The Mayor ducked under his desk, trying to hide.

"Why are you shouting?" Mojo asked.

Ms. Bellum replied, "To give Blossom time..."

"...to do *this*!" Blossom said, kicking a waste-basket so that it smacked Mojo in the ankle and made him trip.

"*Ow!*" exclaimed Mojo. "That hurt! And I have lost track of the person I intended to kidnap! Where is the Mayor? And where is the secret paper that you gave the Mayor?"

"The Mayor's not hiding under the desk!" came the Mayor's voice from under the desk.

"It's none of your business where the Mayor is," answered Blossom, "just like it's none of your business what's written on the paper I gave him..."

"...which is only the Professor's secret family recipe for sugar cookies, anyway," offered the Mayor helpfully.

"The only thing you need to worry about," Blossom added, taking firm hold of Mojo, "is where I am taking you."

"And that will be to jail!" said Ms. Bellum firmly.

Continue on page 64.

Mojo Jojo decided he would command the Talking Dog to obey him. Mojo landed his flying car and strode over to the Talking Dog.

"Listen to me, you miserable mutt," Mojo said. "I am Mojo Jojo, greatest of all monkey supervillains, and I command you to obey me."

The Talking Dog was so astonished, he sat quietly, with his mouth open, staring at the villain.

Good, thought Mojo. *The Talking Dog is in awe of my magnificent might.*

"Now, answer your master," Mojo said. "What is on the paper that Bubbles gave you? What secret are you hiding? Tell me! I command you to speak."

So the Talking Dog spoke...at the top of his lungs. "Help!" he yelled. "Help, Powerpuff Girls! It's Mojo Jojo!"

In an instant, Blossom, Buttercup, and Bubbles, who had heard the Talking Dog with their super-hearing, zipped to the scene. Before Mojo could even protest, the Girls surrounded him.

"Oh, thank goodness you're here, Powerpuff Girls," said the Talking Dog. "Mojo was trying to steal the paper Bubbles brought me!"

"Bad monkey! You shouldn't be mean to other animals," scolded Bubbles.

"What I don't get," added Buttercup to Mojo, "is why you would want to get your hands on the Professor's new formula for flea powder!"

Continue on page 41.

Mojo Jojo decided to keep following Bubbles. He was sure that if the Professor's paper was important, Bubbles wouldn't have given it away. Besides, it wasn't worth Mojo's trouble to plot against the inhabitants of a measly secret club. He wanted to defeat a Powerpuff Girl!

Bubbles began flying faster and faster, and soon she was way ahead of Mojo.

"Curses!" Mojo cried. "What is that little brat up to now?"

Mojo realized that Bubbles was headed to Pokey Oaks, where she and her sisters went to school. The monkey supervillain put his flying car into its highest gear, determined to keep on following Bubbles until he got what he was after.

Continue on page 38.

If I destroy the lab, I might accidentally ruin something valuable that I would rather steal later, Mojo thought. *But if I ruin their home, then The Powerpuff Girls will not have a beautiful place to live in anymore. And then they will be sorry that they did not give the paper to me, Mojo Jojo!*

"Give me that paper," Mojo said, "or you will be saying good-bye to your sofa, farewell to your television, and *adios* to your prized collection of TV Puppet Pals drinking glasses!"

"You're not getting your hairy paws on that paper, Mojo," Blossom replied. "It's the secret formula for Chemical X, and we promised the Professor we'd protect it from creeps like you!"

"Then prepare to face the wrath of Mojo Jojo!" Mojo yelled.

Mojo ran out of the lab and upstairs into the main part of the house. Mojo aimed his pocket laser in every direction. But before any of the laser beams could strike, The Powerpuff Girls were there, using their super-speed and super-strength. Bubbles snatched up the cabinet that held her favorite glassware and flew the entire thing out of harm's way. Buttercup picked up the sofa, and Mojo's laser beam passed harmlessly underneath. Blossom grabbed a big, fancy mirror...and reflected one of Mojo's laser beams right back at him.

Before the evil monkey could duck, he was zapped with his own laser beam!

"*Ow!*" Mojo yelped.

Continue on page 41.

Mojo Jojo's attempt to steal the mysterious secret paper had ended in failure. What was worse (for Mojo, anyway), the formula for Chemical X was safe, which meant that the people of Townsville were safe, too!

And so, once again, the day is saved, thanks to The Powerpuff Girls, who always know how to make a monkey out of Mojo!

THE END